台英雙語童詩集
A Collection of Children's Poems
In Taiwanese and English

一欉小花蕊
A Little Flower

李秀
Louise Lee Hsiu

一欉小花蕊

「台英雙語童詩集」出版的頭序

　　平常時愛寫小說佮散文，童詩毋捌想過欲寫。佇一个溫和的黃昏，音樂家黃友棣教授，看著我導兩个小乖乖，佇文化中心的草埕歡喜走相掠，而且嘴裡哼唱一寡外國的童謠，伊沉重按呢講：「你們這些文字工作者，該為下一代寫些童詩，不要老叫他們毫無選擇的接受外來東西。寫出來！我樂意為他們譜曲。」長者諄諄，聽者謹記在心。自按呢，我完全投入毋單是詩、嘛是童心的境界。

　　「童心是人類內心遙遠的故鄉。」真密貼點出我創作童詩的心路過程。文學創作會當抒發理念佮情懷，尤其寫作兒童文學，愈會當將一个人的童心牽勾出來，親像共失落足久的寶物揣轉來身軀邊全款。因此，一片一片的雲彩、一蕊一蕊的花草、一點一點的雨滴⋯化作囡仔時幼柔的目睭所看著的世界。尤其我厝裡彼兩个學琴的後生、查某囝，予我真濟創作的靈感。

　　兒童是人生發展中一个重要的階段。您的幻想、好奇、同情、想像……差不多生活佇家己的天地內面。事實上，兒童本身就是一部真好的文學。譬如，國小低年級的同學，若看會著的、摸會著的，攏真好玄、有趣味，這是一種純真的直接反應，伊袂考慮其他方面的影響。親像風颱來矣，伊袂想著風颱帶來的災害，因為伊毋免上課、爸母毋免上班，閣再講風颱的勢面佮新奇，會當引起伊足大的刺激感。

　　世界在您看來，人參萬物攏是一家。伊看幼星袂振動，嘛會使講是一群無聽話的囡仔，予月娘老師罰徛佇天頂面；雷公

大概予雷兄弟惹受氣才會發赫大的脾氣；小雨點愛四界跳舞蹉跎，有的佇厝頂要飛刀、有的跳落河內游泳、有的淋佇土跤佮花蕊姐仔開講……這款參天地萬物合一的情懷，真正是人生上美妙的時段。

高年級的同學，身心有足大的發展，求知慾增加，理智咧發育，獨立的個性慢慢形成。求知欲、正義感、愛冒險，時常佇生活中展現出來。像「今仔日」、「空氣」、「阮咧彈琴」……等等，就是您的縮影。觀察童心變化，是寫作童詩上大的快樂！這本童詩集起初是用華語創作，其中十二首，黃友棣教授已經譜成曲，予「兒童唱歌得著快樂」是伊上大的向望。

華語版有得著高雄市文藝獎，頒獎時嘛捌佇高雄文化中心予小朋友表演過。評審所講的「這些著作跳出前輩童詩作家的表現手法，具有獨特的創意。」現在經過十幾冬的歲月，我將它翻譯成英文。

續落來，閣予胡長松的「踏入台文，世界會愈曠闊」觀念影響。起先我有翻英文比翻台文閣較簡單的感覺，真歹勢！我是正港的台灣人矣，呔會使有這款想法。宋澤萊嘛按呢講「佇異鄉寫家己的母語，會當消除思鄉的痛苦」。佇溫哥華每一個寒冷的暗暝，我猶閣投入台文的兒童世界，發現用台文書寫真正是貼肉黏骨。用母語寫童詩，是這世人創作過程中上界美好的感動，伊深深挖掘家己生命中存园的詩意，親像遊子佇他鄉遇著久年失散的親人。

然後我以「台英雙語童詩」系列刊登於北美一个文學組織 "Writer's Digest Community"，受著英語世界讀者參作家熱烈的反應。有一个寫小說的美國作家Timothy，伊講讀我的

童詩，予伊想著19世紀一个眞出名的詩人William Blake的詩；閣有另外一个詩人，捌佇咱台灣台北美國學校教過冊，伊講遮的台英童詩是一本會當予台灣囡仔想欲學英文的好教材……這款的呵咾，對我來講眞正是一種額外的鼓勵。

另外我特別愛感謝澤萊兄，因爲伊蹛的所在袂當買著適合的字典，所以叫長松兄佇高雄寄字典來溫哥華予我，我講郵費傷貴矣，等我轉去台灣才講，長松講「佮作家的作品相比，郵費無要緊啦！」即馬我已經漸漸看著五彩的春光矣，毋單台文的代誌，閣有友情的感動。

這本台英童詩集有28首，向望會當予小朋友、大朋友帶來一寡驚奇，一寡共鳴，知影宇宙萬物之間，攏有值得逐家來啖糝的趣味。

李秀　寫佇加拿大　溫哥華

Foreword

I used to only write essays and novels for adults. I never thought about writing children's poetry. However, that changed when Yu-Di Huang, who is a famous musician, composer and writer from Hong Kong, came to Taiwan to offer his time and expertise to help musical groups. At that time he always encouraged me in both my literary and musical interests as I diligently presided over my telephone company's choir. One warm evening, he discouraged me from singing foreign nursery rhymes with my two children at the Kaohsiung Cultural Center. He said to me, "You are a writer. You have a responsibility to write children's poems for our children to sing in our native language. Don't force them to learn only foreign songs. Write the poems! I will be glad to compose music for them."

I listened to my honored teacher and made a sincere attempt to write children's poetry. Then I became not only involved with the creation of children's poems, but I also discovered my long lost child self and really enjoyed experiencing my innocent side again. When I write that childhood is the remote hometown of the inner human being, I am referring to the process of my children's poetry writing. Even though adult literature expresses the writer's ideas and emotions, writing for children can lead the writer back to childlike innocence and treasured memories of childhood. Thus, elements of nature such

as clouds, flowers and raindrops are the embodiment of a child's vision; furthermore, observing my two children learning to play the piano and the violin also gave me a lot of inspiration to write children's poetry.

A child's development in the first stage of life is rich in fantasy, curiosity, sympathy and imagination. Children often live in their own world. In fact, every child is a literary masterpiece. For example, there is a strong curiosity about what they can see or touch during early childhood. This kind of attitude is why they do not regard things like typhoons as disasters. When the typhoon is coming, they are just excited that they don't need to go to school; Father and Mother don't have to go to work as well. Moreover, experiencing the wild effects of the typhoon stimulates their interest in such a positive way that they dance with joy.

To children, all things under the sun are one. A child looks at the still stars in the sky and has an image of the stars being punished by being forced to stand still by Moon Teacher because they are a group of disobedient children. Children hear the sound of thunder and the thunder is personified as Thunder Father; maybe Thunder Brothers have provoked their father to anger. Looking at small raindrops, children may say that some raindrops play a warrior's game on the roof as they whip each other with their crystal bead bodies, and some raindrops jump into the river to go swimming, but as they all swim together, they are unable to know who is who. These kinds of naive images arise from this most wonderful period of life.

When children reach adolescence (between the ages of 11 and 13), they experience big changes in their physicality and spirituality, such as an increase in intellectual curiosity, more independence, a sense of justice, etc. The poems, "Today", " Air", "Playing Our Music" and so on are expressions of these new interests. Observing childhood changes and writing them down is a fantastic experience.

I wrote these children's poems in Chinese over a decade ago. Among these Chinese poems there are twelve that have music composed for them by Dr. Yu-Di Huang. Getting children to sing merrily is his greatest desire. Actually these melodies were performed by a children's choir when I was awarded a Children's Poetry Prize for this book at the Kaohsiung Cultural Center.

On the other hand, even though I am a Taiwanese writer, I never thought about translating the poems into Taiwanese. I always had this idea that translating into English is easier than translating into Taiwanese. Shame on me! I am really a Taiwanese writer. How dare I get this idea!

Recently, I was in touch with Tiong-Siong Oo, a Taiwanese novelist whose articles are written in Taiwanese. He said that if I go to the world of Taiwanese language, I will find a remarkable vision. Of course, I appreciate this wonderful statement and

want to be in the world of my mother language. Additionally, another famous Taiwanese writer, Tik-Lai Song, said to me, "Writing in your mother language is a good way to solve homesickness in a foreign country." It is true that both writers' encouragement has brought me back to the marvelous world of the Taiwanese language. Now that I have translated these children's poems from Chinese into Taiwanese, I feel like a joyful breeze is playing the musical ripples of my mother tongue upon my heart.

Translating my poems into English was also a great challenge. However, when I finished my English translation of my children's poems, I posted them on the website of the North American "Writer's Digest Community", and I received a lot of positive responses to the poems.

Now I have translated my poems into both Taiwanese and English so that more children can enjoy them. It is my great hope that my poetry in some way reflects the nature of childhood.

Louise Lee Hsiu
January 2011

目錄 Contents

一樣小花蕊
A Little Flower

討債

雨水母仔！汝是毋是
無閒咧洗衫
袂記得關水道頭

日頭爸仔！汝是毋是
無儉電火的習慣
開赫大粒的電火泡仔

冷風叔仔！汝嘛真心適
天氣己經有夠爽快
但是汝閣愛開冷氣吹袂停

風颱伯仔！汝閣較痟
風微微仔吹來上界四序
汝閣愛開赫強的電風一直吹

我看恁實在足無站節
老師見若講一遍
我就養成毋通討債的好習慣

Wasting

Rain Mother!

Are you too busy washing clothes

And forgetting to turn the faucet off?

Sun Father!

Don't you want to save your light?

It is too bright for me today.

Winter Uncle! You are so silly!

The weather is cold enough

But you still turn on your air conditioner.

Typhoon Uncle! You are also crazy!

A soft breeze is comfortable

But you still want to turn on your biggest and strongest fan

You all really waste a lot of energy!

After my teacher taught me only once

I know the right way to save.

蝴蝶結

阿母欲掠一隻足媠的花蝴蝶
囥佇我粉紅仔色的衫
通好導（chhoa7）我去街仔路耍

掠了閣再掠
看著真媠的花蝴蝶
直欲停佇阿母的手蹄頂
攏予我跳來跳去
驚甲伊
毋是這爿的翅仔傷長
就是彼爿的翅仔傷短
阿母一放手
伊就飛走矣

阿母叫我乖乖徛予正
我連鞭徛甲定定毋敢振動
了後阿母真正掠著
一隻足大閣媠的花蝴蝶
囥佇我粉紅仔色的衫
阮就做夥去街仔路蹉跎矣

Butterfly Bow

Mother wants to catch a beautiful butterfly

To put on my pink dress

That I'll wear on our stroll down the street

My mother chases and chases

Until a butterfly

Is caught in my mother's clever hands

But I am always swaying

Frightening the butterfly

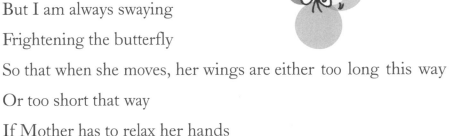

So that when she moves, her wings are either too long this way

Or too short that way

If Mother has to relax her hands

Butterfly flies away quickly

Mother wants me to be an obedient child

I stand still and move less

Finally, Mother catches

A big beautiful butterfly

That becomes a bow tie on my pink dress

And our stroll begins

小雨點

彼日
天頂雄雄變色
恁一个一个相招離開厝
做夥激做水晶柱仔
四界溜溜走假若欲去佗位開同樂會

有的佇厝頂耍飛刀
刮甲水晶珠仔輾過來閣輾過去
有的跳落河底泅水
泅甲分袂出你我伊
有的淋佇塗跤佮花蕊姐仔談天說地
講甲心花逐蕊開甲紅紅紅

恁耍甲無暝無日
耍甲半小死了後想欲轉去厝
無半點元氣閣毋知厝佇佗位
按呢是欲按怎有才調轉去厝歇睏咧

Little Raindrops

That day

The weather suddenly changes

The little raindrops are leaving home one by one

As they leave they change their bodies into many crystal pillars

Going everywhere and dancing happily in the air

Some raindrops play a warrior's game on the roof

Whipping each other with their crystal bead bodies

Some jump into the river to swim

They all swim together unable to know who is who

Some sit on the ground to chat with sister flowers

They talk with others joyfully

They play as much as possible

Until they feel tired and want to go home

But they have lost their energy

And how do they go home after they have lost their way?

培墓

阮提一寡牲禮佮花
來到阿公汝的厝
逐冬這个時陣
攏來遮揣汝開講

即馬汝毋知去佗位
厝邊糞埽滿山墘
埕內埕外草籬四界旋
趕緊清氣汝厝的四邊
汝若轉來就知影阮骨力摒掃過

阮恬恬坐佇門口等汝
逐家講起汝以前種種的形影
即馬無阮佮汝作伴
毋知汝過了按怎

Tomb Sweeping Day

Bringing some gifts and flowers

We go to visit you, our dear grandfather

We must come here once a year

To chat with you

You aren't at home

Under your roof there is a mess of grasses and flowers

And the yard is muddy, too

We help by trimming overgrown trees and cleaning the yard

To give you a surprise

We sit in silence

In front of the door to wait for you

Without us accompanying you

We don't know how you'll get here alone

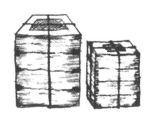

日頭已經欲漸漸落山矣
阮閣愛趕去別位
阿公汝若轉來
一定知影阮有來過

實在行袂開跤
姑不而衷先講一聲再會
明年阮一定會閣再來看汝
阿公呀！彼个時陣
拜託汝毋通閣無佇厝裡

The setting sun is already down

We need to go to another place

When you come back home

You must know we were here to visit you

We are unwilling to part with you

We look back at your home again and again

Next year we will visit you again

Remember, Grandpa, at that time

You need to be at home to wait for us

果子佮其他

蓮霧毋是鈴噹仔

一葩一葩粉紅仔色的鈴噹仔
上愛揣風共伊叮噹響袂煞
但是蓮霧上愛恬靜過活
無愛風來吵吵鬧鬧

葡萄毋是玻璃珠仔

一粒一粒愛耍的玻璃珠仔
上愛輾來輾去走袂停
但是葡萄慣勢佮兄弟姐妹倚靠做夥
無愛予人輾過來閣輾過去傷精神

Fruits and Others

Bells / Bell Apple

A string of small pink bells

Look for the wind to make the sound of ding dong

But apples like peaceful quiet

We don't need the wind to ding dong

Marbles / Grapes

A group of playful marbles

Like the noise of pushing back and forth

But grapes always stay close to each other

Keeping silently softly together

西瓜毋是球

一粒一粒愛走跳的大皮球
上愛揣人共伊拍來拍去
但是西瓜欣羨予人扶來扶去
無愛隨在予人踏過來閣踏過去

楊桃毋是天星

一个一个愛出風頭的天星
上愛懸懸掛佇天頂閃熠
但是楊桃佮意予人清芳退火
無愛懸懸掛佇天頂予人摸袂著

Ball / Watermelon

Big mischievous balls

Look forward to being bounced

But watermelons just like to stay cool

We don't want to be bounced and like to be patted instead

Stars / Star fruit

A series of stars are always showing off

Hanging high in the sky

But star fruit only want to feel good

We don't want to show off in the sky

一枝粉筆

老師來矣，伊上歡喜
伊會使佇黑板談天說地
天文、地理、科學、藝術
假若無一項伊袂曉的

伊干單上煩惱一項代誌
就是予老師大力擲出去
了後伊遵照老師指示的方向
摔落佇咧講話的學生仔身軀頂
予怹雄雄驚一越

伊希望智識的種籽佇心內發芽
予逐家有一日真正發芽開花
若學生有才調吸收所有的道理
就算伊一分一分消瘦落肉
閣一絲一絲予人磨到無身屍
猶甘願滿足伊有身軀通好奉獻

A Piece of Chalk

Chalk is happiest when the teachers come to him

Because he can chat about all sorts of subjects

Such as astronomy, geography, science and art

Chalk knows whatever you want to know

Chalk doesn't like to do just one thing

When he is called on by the teacher

And he needs to follow the teacher's orders

So Chalk hits the students chatting in class

To give them a big shock and stop their talking

Chalk hopes the seed of wisdom grows in students' minds

And they can improve their studying a lot

Students want to learn about everything from Chalk

Even though every moment he becomes thinner and smaller

At the cost of his life

He still enjoys his work

一欉小花蕊

一欉驚惶的小花蕊
佇狂風暴雨的凌治中走投無路
伊一心一意想欲轉去厝走避
但是大滴大滴的雨水阻擋伊的路
風大港大港共伊刁工掠牢咧
害伊毋知欲按怎脫離災厄
伊像新婦仔浸佇塗跤予人蹧躂

好佳哉！阿母隔工導(chhoa7)日頭來看伊
伊趕緊投入阿母的攬抱裡
撒奶揉呀揉
揉過昨昏的驚惶
揉過昨昏的委曲
伊閣再恢復以前的嬌軟佮美麗

A Little Flower

A frightened little flower

Has been struggling against a violent storm

She wants to go home

But the rain hides the way home

And the wind blows her back

She is so scared that she is crying her eyes out

She looks like a poor new student who is being insulted by others

Fortunately, Mother draws out the early sun to visit her

She runs in a great hurry to throw herself in Mother's arms

Wanting to be spoiled and comforted

After getting away from yesterday's storm

And warming herself in her mother's love

She becomes beautiful again

樹公仔

樹公仔上界爽勢

無愛佮別人相借問

一句話攏無愛講

老神在在徛佇遐

看橋跤溪水直直咧流

看橋頂汽車人陣咧吵鬧

予人臆袂出伊是咧想啥

但是樹公仔界專情

獨獨對風媽有感情

便若風媽佇遠遠來欲揣伊開講

伊就開始搖來搖去準備歡迎的形

風媽到位伊就現出歡喜的形四界搖

搖到無暝無日

假若瘖的閣一直那嘎嘎叫袂停

Grandpa Tree

Grandpa Tree is an arrogant guy

Nobody can get him to look at them

He never says anything

He stays quiet as he stands there

Looking at the bridge over the flowing water

Watching for heavy traffic

Nobody knows what he's thinking about

But Grandpa Tree is faithful in love

He only adores talking with Grandma Wind

When Grandma Wind is coming

He gets very excited

Waving his arms and stamping his feet

He cannot stop chattering away joyfully

He sounds like a madman as he yells happily

愛的歌聲

阿母！

汝若是大地，我就是天頂的雨

無論我落偌濟抑是偌少

汝攏笑咪咪表示無要緊

一點仔都袂受氣佮棄嫌

無時無刻踮佇遐等待我

阿母！

汝若是大海，我就是半空中的海鳥

隨在我自由飛踅四界溜溜走

等我飛到無氣無力跤酸手軟

汝曠闊佮柔軟的手抱心

一分一秒隨時欲攬抱我

阿母！

汝若是橋，我就是橋跤的流水

我欲無暝無日守佇汝的身軀邊

誠誠實實閣叮叮噹噹欲對汝講

我愛汝！我愛汝！

Song of Love

Mother!

If you are the earth, I am the rain in the sky

I pour the rain to earth; whether heavy or light

You always accept me

Never complain to me

And you welcome me every time

Mother!

If you are the sea, I am a seagull

I can feel free flying and wandering around everywhere

When I feel completely exhausted

I want a big soft hug from you

And you welcome me every time

Mother!

If you are a bridge, I am the running water under the bridge

I will always accompany you

As I murmur and gurgle to say

I love you! I love you!

A Little Flower 一欉小花蕊

鬱卒的天星

天星是一陣無聽話的囡仔
想欲落來自由的土地行行咧
但是予月娘老師罰徛佇天頂
目睭三不五時偷偷仔振動一下
但是身軀一點仔攏毋敢徙走

汝看！汝的好朋友火金姑
快快樂樂飛到西飛到東
有時好心閃燈火照人的路
有時走去佮樹伯仔扭關係
有時會參花姐仔跋感情

天星呀天星
以後上好做一个聽話的囡仔
到時汝若真正會當落來土地
不但(m̄-nā)會當佮火金姑全款好耍
到時咱做夥鬥陣來四界蹙跎

Unhappy Stars

The stars are not obedient children

They desire to come down and wander around freely on Earth

But Moon Teacher forces them to stand in the sky

Sometimes they dare to move their eyes

But they don't dare move their bodies

Look! Your firefly friends

Fly everywhere happily

Sometimes giving their light to people

Sometimes playing with Uncle Trees

Sometimes talking to Sister Flowers

Oh! My dear stars

You should become obedient children

If you come down to Earth

You could be like the firefly

Then you and I could become friends and play together

今仔日

透早日頭漸漸光起來
慢慢結束昨昏的暗暝
拍散分開晉前的茫霧
但是！我！實在眞愛睏

爸母疼惜的心佮催趕的聲
予我搣開陷眠愛睏的目睭
激力舉頭向日頭予爸母看
去學校的跤步假作信心滿滿

老師徛佇臺仔頂耐心的教示
加減拍開我茫茫渺渺的記智
同學互相看樣比賽啥人較巧
予我想欲知影的代誌愈來愈濟

一大堆的功課我需要趕緊跤步
早轉厝做功課早會當出來蹉跎
今仔日的課業應該今仔日做了
明仔載閣有明仔載的新課業

Today

Dawn breaks

Closing the endless curtain of night

Spreading the misty fog before daytime

But I still want to sleep

Yet my loving parents hurry me

As I open my sleepy eyes

I get up to meet the sun and let my parents relax

And go to school pretending to be full of confidence

Listening to my patient teachers' lessons

My confused thoughts gradually go away

Though my classmates may be smarter

My desire for knowledge grows every day

I have a lot of homework, so I hurry my way home

The faster I do my homework, the earlier I can go outside to play

Teacher said that today's homework must be done today

Because tomorrow there will be more

烏暗的雲

烏暗的雲
今仔日是按怎遮爾無閒
假若有啥物大代誌欲發生
今仔日是按怎無穿彼領白婿衫
敢是汝阿母提去洗

烏暗的雲
汝是毋是予老爸天公伯仔處罰
無歡喜所以顯出烏暗的面腔
拜託汝莫受氣今仔日是我的生日
我有足濟朋友相招欲來阮兜蹉跎

哦！原來汝是欲去耍水
汝實在無界好參詳
汝看！汝潑水潑甲滿四界
阮會予汝害甲悽慘落魄
我的生日就無啥物心適矣

Grey Clouds

Grey clouds!

Why you are so busy today?

Is a big event happening?

Why didn't you wear your beautiful white robes today?

Is it possible your mother took them away?

Gray clouds!

Are you being punished by your father?

Are you so mad at him that you show your miserable faces?

Today is my birthday, please don't be angry

I have many friends visiting me to celebrate

Oh! I see, you want to play with water

You are not a good listener

Look! You not only flood the world

But you also make us very wet

And now my birthday will not be happy

寂寞

阿爸！汝敢會當佮我耍一下？
袂使得，阿爸欲愛去上班
叫阿母陪汝蹉跎啊

阿母！汝陪我蹉跎一下好無？
無閒啦，阿母即馬欲去菜市仔買菜
叫阿姐導(chhoa7)汝去街仔路踅踅咧

阿姐！汝導(chhoa7)我去街仔路踅踅咧敢好？
那有可能，阿姐欲考試即馬愛準備
汝袂曉家己一个人耍哦

好啊！我只好家己一个人耍矣

Lonely

Daddy! Would you please play with me?

No, I want to go to work

Let Mama play with you

Mother! Would you please play with me?

No, I want to go grocery shopping

Let Sister play with you

Sister! Would you please play with me?

No, I want to get ready for school

You play by yourself

Okay! All I can do is play by myself!

狗蟻食我的餅

狗蟻呀！狗蟻！
恁這站雄雄是想著啥物
請問恁相招是欲去佗位
恁逐个親像有受過訓練
無糾察隊會當排甲退四序！

嘿！嘿！
汝這隻請出來這爿一下
害矣！這聲陣頭亂去矣
恁凡勢想講你是欲偷走
我想汝較緊轉去較妥當
予汝的仝伴安心莫煩惱！

哇！哇！
彼頭閣來遮呢濟的朋友
恁是欲去參加啥物同樂會
遐一定是一个好耍的所在
哪會按呢？哪會按呢？
遐是我旦才招阿母買的餅
無經過我的同意就咧偷食！

Ants Eat My Biscuits

Little ants!

What are you suddenly thinking about?

Where do you want to go?

You have no school discipline

But you all line up very well

Hi little guy!

Could you please rest for a while?

Oops! The line is messy when you go away

Your friends might see that you have gone

You must go back quickly

So they won't worry about you

Wow! Wow!

There are so many more friends coming!

Are they headed somewhere to enjoy a party?

It must be a fun place to go

Oh! No! What are you doing now?

Those are my favorite biscuits

My mother just bought them for me, but you are eating them all up!

月娘

月娘是愛嬌的姑娘
共家己粧甲嬌噹噹

月娘欣羨鬧熱驚孤單
定定招天星來佮伊作伴

月娘上驚孤單閣愛風騷
時常佮雲姐仔掩咯雞走相掠

月娘不止仔愛變猴弄變來變去
有時目眉有時芎蕉有時閣大碗公

月娘雖然有赫濟出頭但是嘛真驚歹勢
日頭想欲佮伊約會，毋過伊攏毋敢出面

月娘實在真趣味，但是不時攏懸懸掛佇天頂面
隨在我頷頸伸長長，跤尾躡懸懸，按怎都唗袂著伊

Moon

Moon longs to be beautiful
She always dresses up

Moon is afraid to be alone
She needs stars to be with her

Moon likes to play games
She always plays hide-and-seek with the clouds

Moon plays with magic
She sometimes becomes an eyebrow, a banana or a big bowl

Moon is too shy to go on a date with Sun
When Sun wants to see her, she disappears

Moon is very interesting, but she always hangs too high in the sky
Even when I stretch my neck or stand on tiptoe, I can't kiss her

風颱

風颱伯扎雨水嬌仔
講欲來就真正來矣
阮猶未請恁坐落來
就大範大範衝入內

雖然恁按呢真毋知禮數
但是我毋免去學校讀冊
阿母參阿爸毋免去上班
阿媽毋免去菜市仔買菜
我暗歡喜逐家攏佇厝內

我閣較欣羨恁有赫大的本事
共一塊一塊的厝瓦掀夯起來
一欉一欉硬磕磕的老樹公仔
嘛著聽恁的指揮拼命拋輾斗
愛恁來我才會當看這款風景

Typhoon

Uncle Wind brings Auntie Rain

You came in just as the radio was reporting you

We weren't prepared for you and have no place for you to sit down

You arrived suddenly and forcefully to visit us

It is okay, even though you are so impolite

I don't want to go to school

My mother and father don't want to go to work

And my grandma doesn't to go shopping

I am so happy we are all finally together at home

And I really admire your powerful energy

You can easily lift all the roof tiles one by one

You give orders to old diehard trees as well

They are obedient to your way and turn their somersaults

I enjoy these funny things when you are here

我足想欲去外口好好參恁耍一下
但是廣播電臺講恁漸漸欲離開矣
那會干單來一工爾爾就緊欲轉去
大人討厭恁但是我感覺恁真心適
等待有一工恁會當閣再來行行咧

I long to go outside to play with you

But the radio says you are ready to go away

Why do you only come here for one day?

Although the grown-ups don't like you, I like you so much

I am waiting for you to come again

驚惶

阿叔上愛講鬼仔故事
伊用嘴講手嘛有動作
阿姐聽甲耳仔趴趴
我是愛聽毋過心會驚

佇四界暗摸摸的時陣
我毋敢家己一个人睏
恐驚半暝鬼仔來揣我
阿姐笑我驚死無路用

見若我佮伊冤家了後
伊就講無愛陪我睏矣
害我毋敢無聽伊的話
我是驚伊抑是驚鬼呢？

Scared

Uncle likes to tell us a ghost story

Both his mouth and his hands are busy

My sister is very interested in hearing it

I am afraid of the ghost but I want to listen too

When it is dark outside and inside

I don't dare sleep alone

I am scared that the ghost might come at midnight

My sister laughs at me because I am a chicken

If I quarrel with her

She will say she doesn't want to sleep with me

I have to listen to her

I don't know who scares me most, my sister or the ghost?

佮阿母買物

陪阿母去衫仔店買衫
阮遮摸摸--e，遐看看--e
阿母佮意一領足媠的衫
但是店員講出價數的時陣
阿母目頭結一下講傷貴
就牽我的手趕緊欲離開

阿母陪我去冊店看冊
阮遮摸摸--e，遐看看--e
我佮意一套心適的囡仔冊
但是店員講出價數的時陣
哇！這比阿母的衫閣較貴
我欲牽阿母的手趕緊閃開
但是阿母笑咪咪講哪有貴
我若有佮意就共伊買落來

Shopping with Mother

I go with my mother when she shops

We walk around and around many stores

My mother likes to buy beautiful clothes

When the salesman tells her the price of the clothes

My mother says it is too expensive

And then we run away

My mother goes with me to the bookstores

We walk around and around many stores

I feel happy when I see a beautiful fairy tale collection

When the salesman tells me the price of the book

I say it is more expensive than my mother's clothes

I want to leave with my mother

But my mother says it is not too expensive

If I want it, I can buy it

雷公

雷公扎熠爁雄雄熠落來
是毋是雷媽惹伊受氣
抑是雷兄弟做歹代誌
伊需要喝赫大的雷公聲

雷公性地驚死人小喝一下爾
天頂婆就一直若咧流目屎
流甲土地滿四界攏澹漉漉
我想伊性地有需要改一寡

好佳哉！天頂婆已經無咧哮矣
但是伊猶原閣咧霆(tan5)雷公聲
害阮小妹驚甲規暝哮袂煞
阿母講伊足過份閣無站節

Grandpa Thunder

Grandpa Thunder brings lightning that comes suddenly

Does Grandma Thunder make him mad?

Or Brothers Thunder make trouble?

He must have lost his temper to yell so loudly

Grandpa Thunder's temper is so terrible

Making Great Aunt Sky cry all day long

Her tears fall down and soak through the ground

I think his temper should be softer

Luckily, now Great Aunt Sky stops crying

But Grandpa's bad temper doesn't stop

It scares my sister who cries all night long

My mother says he wants too much from us

溪水

雖然我予人放捨(sak)流浪
我猶原無一點仔厭氣佮失志

勇敢跁(peh)高跁低一山過一嶺
骨力通過彎彎斡斡的老樹跤邊
綿精綿爛泅過坎坎坷坷的土地
無人會當阻擋我滿腹向望的心

趖趖跳跳
哼哼唱唱
我欲予青山聽
我欲予綠水驚

我當欲快快樂樂泅向大海
曠闊的世界佇遐咧等待我

Brook

Even though I am apart from the rest of the world

I am still not sad or helpless

I'm brave enough to climb over rocks and mountains

I strive to pass many crooked old trees

I work hard to flow through the bumpy land

Nobody can keep me from my dream

I enjoy skipping

And singing songs

Let my voice be heard by the green hills

And make the water shiver

I rush joyfully toward the ocean

A bigger world is waiting for me

惡夢

阿母竟然佮一个查甫人
倚做夥糖甘蜜甜愈行愈遠
看著我親像我參伊無熟似

阿母！阿母！
我就是汝的查某囝矣
汝袂使刁工無愛插(tshap)我
汝講汝永遠就是我的老母
我嘛永遠是汝的心肝寶貝

阿爸！阿爸！
阿母即馬哪會變作按呢
阿爸！阿爸呢?
恁逐家哪會攏變做生份人

毋愛！毋愛！
我是按怎雄雄喝袂出聲
唔…唔…

瑩瑩！起床矣！
阿母！汝應該較早叫人精神

Nightmare

I see my mother with a stranger
Cuddling close together, they walk away
They totally ignore me when they see me

Mother! Mother!
I am your darling Ying-Ying
Why are you neglecting me?
You said you are my mother forever
And I'll always be your pet

Father! Father!
How did Mother become like that?
Daddy! Daddy! Where are you?
You have all changed into strangers

No! No! I don't like this!
How did my voice disappear?
Help me! Help me!

Ying! Ying! Wake up
Mother! You should wake me up earlier!

吵鬧的世間

一欉旦即莩茡(puh-inn2)的小樹
伸出幼幼薄薄的頷頸仔
定定向老樹公仔怨嘆講
遮是一个吵吵鬧鬧的世間

身軀規塗沙粉的老樹嘛有同感
是呀!人就是按呢無站節佮無衛生
無耐性的人騎機車親像痟仔喀喀傱(tsong5)
著猴的司機駛車像火燒尻川黑白霆喇叭
壓霸的人處理代誌著夯刀銃拼甲你死我活

小樹搖頭講遮實在是恐佈的所在
老樹公仔嘴講閣講伊猶原拍拼吸收
位四界各所在溢來的垃圾做予小樹看樣
恬恬伸出青翠的雙手安搭人類匆碰的性地

The Noisy World

The weak young tree
Stretches out his tiny neck
Grumbling to the old tree about
How bad this noisy world is

The dusty old tree also has this feeling
Yes, humans lack respect for us
There are crazy bikers who ride their noisy motorcycles
Impatient drivers who race the cars and honk loudly all the time
Violent humans who attack each other with knives and guns

The young tree covers his ears and says this is such a terrible world
But, even though the old tree sighs deeply, he still works hard
Absorbing polluted air to set a good example for the young tree
And stretching his long green arms to help people feel peaceful

天佮地

一片清氣藍白分明的天
嘛是一幅有夠精彩的圖

阿媽的白頭毛
阿公的薰嘴仔
阿姐芭蕾舞的婿衫
小弟噗噗跳的柴馬
攏總懸懸掛佇天頂遐

天色漸漸暗落來矣
阿媽的白頭毛套散落來矣
阿公的薰嘴仔歕出一輾一輾圓箍仔
阿姐躡跤尾舞來舞去攏舞袂煞
小弟騎柴馬一直噗噗跳
有夠鬧熱的天頂盤

The Sky and the Earth

A blue sky filled with white clouds

This is a fantastic picture

Grandmother's white hair

Grandfather's tobacco pipe

Sister's ballet costume

Brother's wooden horse

Are hanging in the sky

The sky is gradually fading away

Grandmother lets her white hair down

Grandfather lights his pipe to blow out a series of white curls

Sister stands on her toes to dance continuously

Brother jumps on his wooden horse to ride away

What a cheerful sky

日頭落山！月娘出來！
阿媽的包仔頭捋好矣
阿公共薰嘴仔收起來
阿姐共婿舞衫脫落來
小弟的柴馬四肢無力

阿母捧出豐沛的暗頓
逐家拍開溫柔的暝燈
厝內的人佮厝外的天
交接一片四序的天地

The sun is setting and the moon is rising

Grandmother pulls her hair into a lovely bun

Grandfather picks up his pipe

Sister takes off her beautiful dancing costume

Brother is tired of riding his wooden horse

Mother makes a rich dinner

We turn on the night lamp

Out the window and inside the family

What a wonderful sky and earth

白蛇傳

春日的落雨天
阮到電影院看白蛇傳
白蛇會當變做白娘娘
青蛇會當變做青娘娘
蛇遮爾婿毋是驚人的動物

落雨了後的一工
我佮小弟佇後埕耍
當心適時陣草埔內
雄雄趨出一尾蛇來
晉前會驚即馬攏袂驚矣

小青！變予阮看覓
若大聲喝若咧等待
青竹絲會當變婿娘娘
阮的喝聲引起阿母來
伊大聲叫阿爸趕緊出來

The Tale of the White Snake

A rainy day in springtime

We went to see the movie: *The Tale of the White Snake*

The white snake become a white lady

The green snake become a green lady

So the snake was not a terrible animal after all

After one rainy day

My brother and I were playing in the yard

While we were playing joyfully

A green snake suddenly showed up in the thick grass

Now we were not scared anymore

We yelled: Little Green! Please change!

We called and waited for her

To become a beautiful lady

But our loud voices brought our mother

She yelled at Father to come

惢同齊將小青掠起來
我佮小弟攄大目睭咧等候
小青關佇籠仔內趖來趖去
自頭到尾攏無變做青娘娘
原來白蛇傳毋是真正的代誌

They joined forces to catch the snake

We kept our big eyes wide open while we waited

The little green snake was placed in a cage and crawled around

We waited for a long time but Little Green never became

 a green lady

The Tale of the White Snake is not a true story

空氣

天色漸漸暗落來
白雲跳規日的舞
鳥仔飛規日的自由
我要甲規日的疲勞
逐家需要轉去厝歇睏

空氣呀！空氣！
汝敢無厝？汝敢袂疲勞？
無哪會定定佮阮做夥鬥陣
老師講阮的生命袂使無汝
所以汝一分一秒攏袂當歇睏

規日無歇睏敢會使
老師講汝上愛清氣
實在無啥物報答汝
阮儘量毋通製造糞埽
通予汝清氣仔清氣過日子

Air

The sky gradually fades away

The clouds dance all through the day

The birds fly freely all day

I play until I'm tired that day

We all need to rush home to take a rest

Air! Air!

Do you have your own home? Are you tired?

Otherwise you always follow us

Teacher says that our life cannot go on without you

So you can't take a rest any time

You must be very tired if you can never rest

My teacher says that you long for cleanliness

I have nothing to repay you for your hard work

All I can do is try not to get dirty

So a little part of your world will be cleaner

冤家

阿母若拭目屎若講
若無爲著囝伊袂留佇厝
阿爸氣噗噗大聲喝起來
若無後生伊早就離開矣

每擺怹若爲著代誌相冤家
就揉來揉去講攏是爲著我
我變成怹負擔的糞埽物
我定定想欲按怎辦較好

阿爸參阿母閣冤家起來矣
我足想欲藏起來抑是死去
予怹著急四界攏揣無我
我就毋免煩惱怹欲離婚

Quarrel

Mother is crying and says
She would leave this home if they didn't have a child
Angrily, Father says the same thing
If they didn't have a child, he would already be gone

Every time they quarrel
They say it is because of me
I have become their burden
I am always wondering what I can do

Father quarrels with Mother again
I really want to hide somewhere or die
Let them anxiously look for me everywhere
And then I won't need to worry that they will get a divorce

禮物

阿母！
汝直欲轉來矣所以我門無鎖
按呢汝毋免鎖匙就會當入來
淺拖园佇門口汝隨時會當穿
汝講我成績若有進步就是禮物
今仔日有上好的禮物欲送予汝

瑩瑩！
爲啥物門鎖無好勢
歹人入來欲按怎
淺拖嘛烏白园
攏已經六年矣
閣遮爾毋捌（bat）代誌

阿母！
汝莫去股票市場好無
我無愛閣食牛排大頓
嘛無愛電動的蹉跎物
汝的心情若莫無歡喜
我攏會足乖聽汝的話

Gift

Mother!

The door isn't locked so you can come in quickly

I'm setting your slippers down in front of the door

You can put them on at once when you come home

You said if I improve my school scores that is the best gift

I want to present a good gift to you today

Ying-Ying!

Why isn't the door locked?

How could you deal with a bad guy if he came in?

The slippers are not placed the right way as well

Even though you are a grade six student

You act like a younger child

Mother!

Would you please not go to the stock market?

I don't want to have a big meal

And I don't need more electronic toys

As long as you are in a good mood

I will do everything you like

阮咧彈琴

阿母趁阮細漢的時陣
頭腦記智強較好學習
小弟予伊學習小提琴
我四歲的時就彈鋼琴

我上愛「洋娃娃之夢」
只是老師講我的夢娃娃
醒了後的舞步像咧行路
我想欲予伊真正跳起來
不而過我心內干單煩惱
大力水手毋知會過關無

小弟偷偷仔共電視拍開
當等大力水手咧戰鱸鰻
這個時陣門鈴叮噹響起
阮緊關掉電視衝入琴房

Playing Our Music

Mother says that very early on when we are children
We have a strong memory for learning anything
She lets my younger brother learn the violin
And lets me learn the piano when I am four

I like to play *Dolly's Dreaming and Awakening*
But teacher says that my Dolly's dance steps
Are too slow after she wakes up
I do want to make her jump up to dance
But I'm always concerned about what's on TV
If and when Popeye goes on an adventure

Younger brother stealthily turns up the TV
As Popeye heatedly fights the hoodlum
Suddenly the door bell dings dongs
We quietly turn off the TV and rush to the music room

Do Re Mi的旋律
連鞭響到樓梯頭仔
爸母笑咪咪行入門
阮吐舌喘一个大氣
偷做使目尾的笑聲

The melody of Do Re Mi......

Resounds from the top of the staircase

Father and Mother are very happy to enter our room

Younger brother and I breathe hard

We have a secret understanding smile

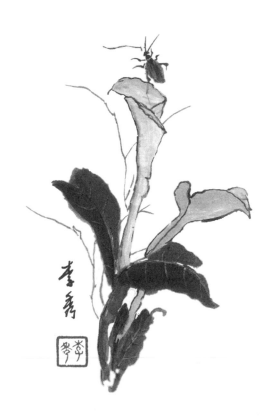

評李秀的台語童詩「天佮地」(華語)

——並論海德格(Martin Heidegger，1889～1976)
「詩意的棲居」　　　　　　　　　　　/ 宋澤萊

【原台語詩】

天 佮 地

一片清氣藍白分明的天
嘛是一幅有夠精彩的圖

阿媽的白頭毛
阿公的薰嘴仔
阿姐芭蕾舞的婿衫
小弟噗噗跳的柴馬
攏總懸懸掛佇天頂趖

天色漸漸暗落來矣
阿媽的白頭毛套散落來矣
阿公的薰嘴仔歎(pun5)出一輾(1in3)一輾的圓箍仔
阿姐躘跤尾舞來舞去攏舞袂煞
小弟騎柴馬一直噗噗跳
有夠鬧熱的天頂盤

日頭落山！月娘出來！
阿媽的包仔頭捋好矣
阿公共薰嘴仔收起來
阿姐共媌舞衫脫落來
小弟的柴馬四肢無力

阿母捧出豐沛的暗頓
逐家拍開溫柔的暝燈
厝內的人佮厝外的天
交接一片四序的天地

一、回到本真的世界

　　李秀要出版童詩了。
　　本童詩原來用北京語書寫，也翻成英語在北美刊物登過。
不論以北京語或英語發表，都獲得高度評價。如今她將這些詩
翻譯成台語，準備以台英雙語問世。
　　台灣人寫詩，只要他本人還能聽說幾句台語，不論用何種
語言書寫，多少都會受制於他的母語，在字裏行間都會散發出
母語的味道，老一輩作家〔日治時代成長過來的作家〕甚至認
為：台灣人寫北京語的文章事實上是另一種翻譯，因為作家先
用台語在內心思考一遍，再用北京語表現出來。我認為年輕一

評李秀的台語童詩「天佮地」(華語)

代作家也許不會有這麼嚴重的翻譯過程，但受制於母語是不爭的事實，那就是為什麼60、70年代鄉土文學裡，黃春明、王禎和的小說會使用那麼多台語辭彙的原因。因此，李秀這些台語詩，不能單純將它當成北京語詩的翻譯，應該說是一種還原，以台語來恢復其本來面目罷了；換句話說她這些台語童詩，在語言上恢復到母語的本眞世界去了。

同時這是一本童詩，是非常特別的一種詩。大致上童詩創作，不能說是大人模仿小孩在寫作。所謂「模仿」應該是和描寫的對象在經驗上完全分離、陌生，再依主觀認定，仿同那個對象來做表現，比如說模仿一只白鶴，展開亮翅的身段；或者是摹仿只百靈鳥，展開我們千迴百折的歌喉，才眞正叫做「模仿」，關鍵是我們本來「不在其內」。但是寫童詩不同，因為大家都曾當過兒童，對童年的人生曾有過種種經驗、覺察、感受、記憶，我們只不過又一度驅遣自己，返回原來有過的世界來進行創作。我們把自己拉回到童年世界，再度感受那個世界的形形色色，再進行書寫。那個世界本來就離我們很近，甚至不到咫尺之遙，只要伸手就可摸到，有時實在太接近了，即使不是寫童詩，還是免不了受他們巨大影響。這就是為什麼觀看超現實主義畫家夏卡爾（Марк Шага́л——白俄羅斯語，1887～1985）和盧梭（HenriRousseau，1844～1910）的作品，會發現他們的畫接近兒童畫的原因。童詩的創作者事實上是將自己再度拉回到一個童年本眞的世界，也就是「在其內」，在那裡從事的一種創作。

所以，李秀的童詩既是在語言上恢復其本眞，同時也在生命上恢復其本眞，以之來進行她的創作，這是李秀個人向著其

本真的工作，恢復其雙重本真的一場運動。

二、天、地、人的三重世界

首先談題目，這首詩題目是：天佮地，即是天空和地面。詩人為什麼要使用這個乍看十分平凡題目，我認為有幾個原因：

第一，因為它的單純性。這是一首童詩，是寫孩童對自身以外的世界感覺。就小孩子而言，世界不可能像大人一樣複雜。大人通常會將周遭分成八荒，甚至剖析成360個向度，以之確定自己存在的方位，以及自己變化多端的視野，這是因為我們的理智發達。然而，小孩不可能如此，它有一定理性程度。但也不是完全沒有理性，它能分高下，並使自己視野達到他所認知的盡處，那就是天空和地面，並停留在那個盡處，因為在盡處之外，小孩就不知道那是什麼。而在那盡處做種種的夢想，也可以說，天和地就是小孩的視野和思想的極盡處，以之做為小孩整個視野的概括。所以詩人用了這個題目，使詩的範圍有所規定，避免內容的無限性和漂泊性。詩人擺明告訴我們，她就只寫小孩對天空和地面的感覺。

第二，詩人用天和地這種小孩的極盡視野，暗示她是在寫小孩的一個完整的封藏世界。天地交接，形成一個圓球體，最起碼是半個圓球。在這個世界裡，小孩有他一己的世界，是我們很難介入和改變的。那是小孩的一切，不被奪取，也不會流失，是完整的。詩人先暗示，這是一個完滿的世界，然後再為我們揭蔽。

第三，事實上，天和地之間，還有一個小孩的自我存在。這個小孩以心靈的自由，吸收了天地於自身的存在裡面。她以小孩為圓心，將天和地納入心中，形成一個太一，變成另一個母親的胎盤或子宮，自從它離開母親以後，它對母親的肚腹還有一種印象，那是它可以安然酣睡的地方。現在，它依然嚮往，因此，就構築另一個肚腹，使它能夠安心地休息。所以詩人暗指，這是一個小孩的另一個母腹，是它在世的居所，以之它可以安然棲居。

　　第四，假如我們不知大人的世界，也就不知什麼是小孩的世界，它們形成一個相對性的結構，彼此召喚。因此詩人寫詩的目的，在於告訴我們，小孩世界與大人世界存在著多少的距離，在這個距離裡，大人所得到的不會只是光榮或驕傲，更多可能是一種喪失。我們喪失了母親的子宮、保障、安全，也喪失小孩的太一世界，我們流落四方，無家可歸。詩人以這種距離，召喚曾經失去的，帶來無邊的惆悵和嚮往，因此，這首詩就不再是一首童詩，而是每個大人紓解鄉愁和傷慟的一首詩。

　　實際上，從詩人的題目看來可能有更多內涵或歧義〔Ambi-guity〕，有關這方面我們要在這裡就打住，另外來看看有關本詩的內容和詩人修辭的手段。

三、內容和修辭

　　先來看第一段：「在那高高的頭頂上，只是一片乾淨的、沒有過多東西的藍白分明天空；但是從白雲的形狀來看，它又是一幅多麼精彩的畫。」這些意思，被寫成短短的兩句話：「

一片清氣藍白分明的天 ／ 嘛是一幅有夠精彩的圖 。」詩人在這裡先佈置了一個舞台——藍天，備後續演員演出空間。這個空間是單純的，就只有藍天。很像一個極端的現代劇場，背景除單一的大片原色之外，沒有其他。詩人在這裡暗示，這是由於小孩喜歡單一、不喜歡複雜。相對於大人世界，小孩永遠是單純的。任何童歌，歌詞都不會太長，而且小孩喜歡重複和押韻，一再唸同樣的幾句話，樂此不疲，這是因為重複就是音樂。太過複雜東西，將會使小孩失去韻律感的快樂。儘管舞台只有一片藍天，可是小孩一定會一看再看，並傾注所有的心，在那裡跑來跑去，甚至飛躍奔馳，產生許多無聲的愉快律動。不過這首詩主要不是寫藍天，藍天不是主角，詩人就沒有必要書寫藍天帶給小孩多大的愉悅，詩句就只是用了藍天一色來做表達。

接著白雲出場，清潔的白雲，就是演員。詩人為何要用「清氣」這個形容詞？這不只是暗示小孩不喜歡太過複雜的東西，同時也暗示小孩的心理是純潔的，不被污染的，一切都還處在天然無邪狀態中。在這裡，白雲不像藍天只是一望無際的不動，當小孩看它時，已經變化許久了，它分開或藕斷絲連，以至造成小孩喜歡的種種圖形，由於形狀個個不同，所以小孩說它們構成了一幅精彩的圖畫。詩人在這裡使用「畫」這個字，將小孩所學習到「畫的世界」投射到白雲，將小孩主觀的心靈世界，疊印在客觀的白雲上面，它的「畫」觀念已經超過平日紙上的作業，而能運用在大自然上，也表示它已能涵納大自然於自己的心靈世界之中，它的心靈已能由狹小的一己世界，通達到外境，能到達物我交融的一個新世界中。「精彩的」這個

形容詞，除說明小孩很喜歡這幅天空的圖畫以外，也暗示它已經有頗為豐富的鑒賞能力。

其次，詩人在這兩行短短詩句中，顯露了使用色彩的能力。「藍」「白」主導了整個畫面。一般來說，大半詩人眼中無色，對顏色使用遲鈍，卻不知顏色會主導詩的氣氛和類型，過多枯黃、黑暗色調會帶來秋冬的印象，終而導致悲劇的後果；反之藍白、朱紅的色調會帶來春夏意境，終而導致喜劇後果。詩人在這方面倒是很內行，「藍」「白」顏色的使用，使她這首詩被界定在喜劇的範圍內，她用色和詩所要表達的愉快、無憂、無邪的境界達到完全的統一，這就是詩人修辭手段的高明。

在這兩句中，詩的結構性相當明顯。一個是天空被分成藍天和白雲的對立結構，彼此可收到陪襯效果，使兩造顯得更為分明；一個是靜〔藍天〕和動〔白雲〕的對立性結構，可以發揮反襯效果，使靜更靜，動更動。結構會形成詩的戲劇性，也使詩的畫面有了立體感。這是詩人另一種高明的修辭法。

這兩句詩是完全的，無法挑出任何的毛病。

再來看第二段：「祖母的白頭髮、祖父的煙斗、姊姊的芭蕾舞衣、弟弟蹦蹦跳的木馬，都高高地懸掛在天空哪兒。」這些意思被寫成：「阿媽的白頭毛／阿公的薰嘴仔／阿姐芭蕾舞的嬌衫／小弟噗噗跳的柴馬／攏總懸懸掛佇天頂遐。」

這段第一次揭開詩人所說的「精彩畫面」，也是眾多塊狀白雲的第一回合演出。原來藍色舞臺是無垠無際，白雲要怎麼表現就怎麼表現，但就在第一次，當這個小孩發現天空形成一個畫面時，它已經有了祖母的白頭髮、祖父的煙斗、姊姊的芭

蕾舞衣、弟弟蹦蹦跳的木馬這些形狀。這一段揭露了詩中所說的「畫」，也就是第一次揭開小孩的整個天空世界。我們說，當小孩在它的目力所及和地方做思考時，也就在進行另一種遊戲〔小孩的活動就是遊戲〕，但是所謂遊戲，也絕非無意義。小孩投射力一向強大，它會用芭比娃娃哭餓來指涉自己哭餓，甚至娃娃穿的美麗衣裳，無非都是投射自己於對象上。在這種情況，白雲就成為它投射的媒介。果然，這些白雲經過投射後，終於產生一番豐富的內涵，它們原來都變成地面上家族成員的物件，而且很清晰指出是哪些物件。白頭髮可以代表祖母，煙斗可以代表祖父，木馬可以代表弟弟……雖然這是一個高高懸掛的天空世界，卻與地面的世界一模一樣，原來是一個由家人構成的世界。小孩複合了天和地，形成一個圓滿封藏的家族世界，小孩就置身其間，成為家族成員圍繞保護的個體，且安然地棲居在這個世界之中。短短 4 行文字，詩人為我們揭蔽，叫我們看見小孩世界裡具體的內容。可說是乾脆明確，毫不拖泥帶水。

在修辭法上，它先使用了省略法，換句話說，詩人認為小孩的世界可能比她所寫的還多。因為，真正有多少白雲的形象，是不容易斷定的。也許還包括了「母親的」「阿姨的」「叔叔的」……，只因為這是一首詩，不能通通展示，詩人就將其餘的刪掉。我們可以設想，還有更多的形狀沒有被表達，它蘊藏在詩本身裡頭，這是毫無疑問的。

另外，作者又使用修辭上的「排列法」，將這些意象並比排列。詩人為什麼要這樣排列？這裡最少有作者兩個目的：第一目的，是造成音樂性：這一段的前兩句中，都是 6 個字，排

成「○○的○○○」；後兩句是 8 個字，排成「○○○○○的○○」，結果由於句法字數的重複，帶來了音樂性。在前面提過，小孩喜歡重複唸誦簡單句子，因為重複會帶來音樂和律動，可以看出，詩人在這裡正確把握了小孩的天真和童趣，深入了解小孩的語言習慣，所以她才使用了這種排列法，這一點說明了詩人對小孩有高超理解力。

第二目的，是激發我們回到童年世界之中：這些意象對於大人來說是永遠的鄉愁，當我們長大在大腦當中，已很難蜂擁出現這些意象，它們離我們越來越遠，甚至被遺忘，當看到詩人把這些東西湊合在一起時，我們先感到驚訝，接著就被帶回到孩童境況中，回到我們鄉愁的極深地帶。這是詩的一種奧秘：當詩人表達一個境界時，憑藉的不是一種說明或敘述，而是「呈現」那些意象在我們眼前，當讀者接觸到這些物象時，我們和詩人同樣的感情經驗就被召喚而出，還原到詩人所要傳達的境界，造成詩人和讀者在境界上的合一。諾貝爾文學獎的英國詩人T.S.艾略特說這叫做「客觀投影objective correlative」。在這裡，詩人故意密集呈現蜂擁的意象，叫我們剎那回到童年歲月裡的家人世界，那就是故鄉，也是另一個母腹。這是詩人在意象運用的一種勝利。

再談第三段，是寫白雲變形的盛況：「天色逐漸暗轉向昏黃，天空的白雲圖形也轉變了。祖母的白頭髮慢慢地披散下來了；祖父的煙斗開始冒出一團團的圓圈圈；姊姊開始撐直後腳跟不停地的跳著她的舞步；小弟騎在木馬上一直跳動……真是熱鬧的天空。」這些意思被寫成：「天色漸漸暗落來矣／阿媽的白頭毛套散落來矣／阿公的薰嘴仔歕(pun5)出一輾一輾的圓

箍仔／阿姐蹕跤尾舞來舞去攏舞袂煞／小弟騎柴馬一直噗噗跳／有夠鬧熱的天頂盤。」這六行詩句。

我們知道，白雲在天空不會永遠只是一種圖形，隨著風的吹拂，會不斷變化形狀，只是有時變化得較快或較慢而已。估計這個小孩所看到的變化應該不會太快，所以小孩可以完全掌握它們的變化過程，而且終至於延續到黃昏。

「時間」在這裡是一個要素。對於大人來說，時間當然被分成過去、現在、未來，唯側重何者，依個人的性情來決定。對一個極端盼望著未來的人而言，一切皆未來，他的時間可能通通變成未來，時間觀念無非就是過去的未來、現在的未來、未來的未來。對於過去太過重視的人而言，他時間觀念就變成過去的過去、現在的過去、未來的過去。對於聖奧古斯丁而言，一切皆現在，時間就變成過去的現在、現在的現在、未來的現在，因為他有不堪回首的過去，對未來也不太能把握。只有神的心中無時間，因為上帝看千年如一日，一日如千年。小孩呢？當然不至於沒有過去、現在、未來之分，但應該比較靠近神這邊，時間劃分不是深刻的，在時間上它還沒有學習太多的分裂手段，時間可能只是一種無限的綿延。也因此，黃昏對於悲觀的大人來說，意指著時間是一種即將來到的結束，是一個悲劇的即將臨到。大人會認為黃昏的天空應該是白雲的火葬場，以一場瘋狂的大火，企圖結束所有天空的變幻，接著就一無所有，儘管美麗，終局是悲慘的；一如四季裡的秋天，看著美麗的楓紅，卻想到世間無常。但小孩可能不會這麼認為，因為小孩不太能理解「結束」或「死亡」，「空無」在它心靈裡沒有地位，萬物在小孩心靈可能是接近永恆。因此，黃昏的天空

在小孩變成一場喜劇演出的舞台，悲劇性被取消，更且比大白天更加歡喜。

也因此，祖母的白頭髮、祖父的煙斗、姊姊的舞衣、弟弟的木馬……更加擴張它們的活力，在不停變化中，顯得更加活潑。小孩的想像力〔遊戲〕也在這時，發展到最高峰，多麼不同於大人對黃昏的感覺！

在這一段，詩人的修辭法依然是「省略法」「排列法」並用。所得到的效果有如上一段。至於詩人有否使用「比喻法」？這是一個值得探討問題。

如上一段一樣，這一段的修辭，在寫祖母白頭髮這些圖象時，並沒有出現「白雲像是祖母的白頭髮」這類寫法，換句話說，文字並沒有出現「是」「似」「如」「好像」這些字眼。所以要說作者使用比喻法，很有問題。不過一定會有人說，這是詩人把這些字眼隱藏起來，事實上是有做這種比喻的，只是字面上看不到而已，在修辭法上就叫做「轉化」，意思是詩人將白雲的圖形直接轉化成白頭髮這些東西。這麼說當然未嘗不可！但是要注意，小孩的世界並不知道什麼是「比喻」！「比喻」這個東西是大人的分別心的產物，由於過度區分「情人」和「玫瑰」是兩樣東西，大人們才說：「我的情人像一朵紅紅的玫瑰。」小孩可能不會這麼說，我們很少聽到小孩說：「洋娃娃像我。」或者「洋娃娃是我。」它只會說：「洋娃娃。」在幼小心靈可能把洋娃娃和他本人當一物，混在一起，這是完全投射的結果。所以當小孩說：「洋娃娃的衣服破了！」你一定要分清楚它所說的洋娃娃到底是指玩具的洋娃娃，或指它本人！站在這個觀點上，我們就不能說詩人使用「比喻法」。

再來看第四段:「太陽終於在西邊的天際線沉落,月亮出來。祖母的髮髻梳好了;祖父的菸斗也收藏起來了;姊姊的舞衣脫下來了;弟弟的木馬顯得四肢無力。這時,家裡的母親端出豐富的晚餐,大夥兒打開溫柔的燈光,家裡的人與家外的天空交接成一片舒適的天地。」它被寫成「日頭落山!/月娘出來!/阿媽的包仔頭抒好矣/阿公共薰嘴仔收起來/阿姐共媜舞衫脫落來/小弟的柴馬四肢無力/阿母捧出豐沛的暗頓/逐家拍開溫柔的暝燈/厝內的人佮厝外的天/交接一片四序的天地。」這9行句子。

　　時間已經來到了夜晚。對於大人來說這代表了死亡,也就是四季的冬天,一切都歸於空無,黑夜吞噬一切,我們可能對夜空一點都不會眷戀,或者已懶得再察看夜空了,儘管還有月亮。但是小孩不是這樣,他繼續盯住那些圖形努力地觀看。對於那些圖形的消彌,大人們會簡單地說:「它們不在了。」但是小孩不會這麼認為,我已經說過,「空無」在小孩的心靈中沒有地位,「不存在」的觀念還不是那麼發達。這個小孩應該還認為,那些圖形都還存在於天空,只是有些藏起來了,有些還未藏起來罷了。「成為空無」觀念小孩一定想不通,就像小孩之間的捉迷藏,當「鬼」的人不是死了或不存在於世間,而是藏起來了,等一下鬼被抓到,鬼就復活,又變為人了,這是小孩世界的最大奧秘,大人或許難以測量。因此,儘管天空白雲的若干圖形不見,它只是認為「梳好了」「藏起來了」「脫下來了」,並沒有認為歸於空無,明天它們又會在天空裡復活回來;對小孩來說,告訴它火鳳凰的故事是多餘的,因為小孩的世界就是火鳳凰的世界,它通常都棲居在那裡,小孩實在是

伊甸園的生靈。

　　「母親」在這裡顯得重要無比，詩人這時才叫她出現。爲什麼不讓她出現在天空呢？就象徵意義來說，因爲母親就是大地，她立於大地，代表大地，也代表供應一切糧食和世間的溫暖。有了她，就有豐富的晚餐；母親的體溫，使整個夜晚都富足、安全起來。就修辭手段來說，她不可以在前面的詩行就出現，會造成重覆，削減修辭的新奇效果。「燈光」在這裡也出現了，它一方面表示白晝的持續，只是由天上降臨到地面而已；也象徵這是一個澄明之境，是一個發光的境界，就是真理之境，是可靠性十足的境界，既沒有空無，也沒有黑暗。

　　最後兩個句子最重要，小孩總結它此刻的感受，說它置身於一個安然舒適的世界，在這裡天地交接在一起，成了一個圓形。「天地交接」在這裡運用得非常好，表示一個完整宇宙的構成，既在小孩自身之外顯得完全，也於內在心靈中顯得完滿，這個宇宙就是小孩的宇宙，也就是它棲居之所，是它另一個母腹，可以繼續休養生息終至長大成人的地方。最後兩個句子爲全詩畫下完美句點。

　　從修辭手段來看，詩人延續了前兩段的「省略法」「排列法」，額外增加了「象徵法」。在這裡，母親、燈光、晚餐、天地交接都蘊含極深的象徵意義，加重了詩的內在奧義，使詩擺脫了單純兒童詩的限制，進入了形上的範疇，帶來詩的永恆價值，「詩意」在這裡有極高的提升，這就是詩人修辭手段所引發的重大效果。

四、詩意的棲居

存在主哲學家海德格在他晚期思想裏，展開了對現代科技世界的批判，想要使人回到自然中去棲居〔安頓自己的心靈〕。「自然」就是「眞正的存有」，就是「眞理」「一」。

　　他認爲人類本來是自然的一部份，棲居於大地之上。但是人總不以爲他是如此，他一直突出自己，自認是大自然的處理者。因此，當自然不能滿足他時，就以各種方式去處理自然，甚至挑戰她、壓迫她、摧毀她。將萊因河的流水阻斷，使之水位上升，又迫使它激射而下，推動渦輪，生產電力。如此，又不足夠，再以人類的意志，開山闢路，架設電纜電線，強迫電力輸送千哩，抵達家中。如今的世界，所呈現都是科技的意志，只是人的意志，再也沒有其他的存在。人就陷身在虛假的存有〔意志、理性的世界〕中，忘記眞正的存有〔自然、眞理〕。

　　人既然盲目屈從理性、意志、科技，喪失對自然本來的觀照，所得的世界認知，都是一偏之見，人也無法返回自然懷抱之中，終致產生孤立、焦慮、不安，變成無家可歸，流落四方的現代人，成爲不善於棲居〔虛假的存有〕的生靈，十足可歎。

　　那麼，人怎樣才能返回眞正的棲居呢？懂得安身立命之道呢？

　　海德格晚期開始介入藝術和詩的探討，他指出返本歸原之道：人必須要能夠「詩意般地棲居」。

　　「詩意般的棲居」是什麼？這裡指的詩意不是浪漫的詩意，而是形而上的思考。思考什麼？那就人在觀看眼前事物時，能還事物給神〔註：海德格是一個泛神論者〕、給人、給天、

給地。在一次觀照下，將萬物所呈露的神、人、天、地四種要素都觀照出來，人就棲居在這四重性中，達到了詩意的棲居，也就是來到「真正的存有」裡安身立命。

他舉例說：當我們看一個「事務」，不必將它看成是我之外的一個對象，而應該把自己也包括在內，觀看「事務」能展現什麼。每個「事物」都能展現出什麼呢？例如一個陶罐放置在眼前，不必一定把他當「人造的工具」看，可以試想，它之所以為陶罐，是因為它能盛水、盛酒、盛物。水取之於泉石之間，泉石乃根植於天上的雨露和大地之中，所以一個陶罐，已經宿含了天、地這雙重要素。再者，陶罐盛水和食物，乃是為供應人們日常飲用，這就宿含了人的要素。再者盛酒乃是為祭神，此又宿含神的要素。因此，一個陶罐就宿含了天、地、人、神四重性當中。絕非唯科技理性底下的「工具物」可以涵蓋，它乃是蘊含著豐富內含的存有物，蘊含「真理」於其內。

可是，一般人不能夠做到這種關照，因為他們的觀照被理性、意志、科技遮蔽了。只有一種人能夠，那就是詩人。因為詩人總是能夠為神聖的東西命名。那什麼又是「神聖的東西」？那就是事物的本質。什麼又是「事物的本質」？那就是自然。什麼又是「自然」？那就是純粹的存在。什麼又是「純粹的存在」？那就是能「宿含神人天地四重性的存有」，也就是「真正的棲居」，也就是「詩意的棲居」。海德格又有一大堆的名詞，來指稱這種「詩意的棲居」，比如說「無蔽狀態」「純然體驗」「存在的家園」「一」「道」「無〔不是空無〕」「澄明之境」「光亮本身」……名目之多叫人乍舌，但都指「詩意的棲居」。

因此，詩人就是最能和大自然打交道，進入無蔽狀態的人，他應該率先引導眾生，讓眾生都懂得真正的棲居，告別無家可歸的存在。歸結來說，詩作品就是最有效的引導。因為詩就是詩人的語言，當詩完成，詩人離去〔海德格說詩完成時，詩人即行死去〕，語言就會展開「神人天地的四重性」，為觀看的讀者揭蔽，呈露澄明之境。當然不是每一首詩都能夠，乃必須要像賀德靈那種詩人的詩才能夠，里爾克都還不太能夠。可見海德格的所謂「詩人」「詩意」「詩」的標準都很高。不過，海德格也認為不只詩才有詩意，繪畫、雕刻、音樂都是詩，都有詩意，儘管它們的藝術形式不同，但是本質都是一種語言，都是詩，只是詩作品比較純粹而已。可見，「詩意」還不見得很難找到。

　　海德格後期的哲學其實就是教人返回大自然的一種哲學，因為科技只見理性和意志，把神、人、天、地都放逐了，實在是太偏頗。

　　海德格這種思想，在西方人眼光中可能是高明的，因為西方人很少這麼想過。但坦白說，在東方人看來，卻不怎麼高明。這種大自然的哲學〔或者說詩學〕在東方其實非常普遍，而且已成過去。

　　按海德格對詩的要求，我們首先就會想到《楚辭》，像屈原的《離騷》就完全符合海德格的標準，因為天地人神四要素在《離騷》裡都有異於常態的湧動和奔騰。其他包括魏晉南北朝、唐宋、明、清的山水詩，諸如陶淵明、謝靈運、王維、孟浩然和大量的遊仙詩、禪詩，也都能符合，乃至於印度的詩哲泰戈爾的詩更是極端標準。賀德靈的詩儘管被海德格推崇，但

是要勝過東方這些詩人的作品也有所不能。

　　其實，就靈修層次來看，海德格的自然境界還在東方道家、禪宗或印度哲學那種「物我合一」的渾沌世界之下，他的大自然哲學其實是東方世界歷史的陳跡。要把這種境界和詩意在現代世界中復活過來，必然有所不能。海德格也感嘆說：我們可能無法回到那個世界了！

　　再者，「自由表現」乃是藝術的內在和外在的本質，去除自由表現，藝術就會淪亡，除了修辭法則之外，藝術家不被所有的要求所羈縻，海德格終將不能要求詩人或觀賞者用一類觀點來寫詩、看詩。他所謂「詩意」的要求是一個烏託邦，可能沒有任何的現代詩人或藝術家會遵循他所提出的原則。

　　但是，有一種文類或藝術種類可能和海德格的「詩意」的要求非常接近，成為海德格的永遠支持者，那就是童詩或童畫。

　　我們注意到，李秀這首〈天佮地〉，就很符合他的「詩意」要求。這首童詩中，天、地、人、神四要素昭然若揭，四要素彼此呼應，複合成天衣無縫的混圓世界，達至無法再超越的澄明之境。李秀28首童詩幾乎都和這首〈天佮地〉一樣，表達天地人神兒童的存有境界。不但是李秀的童詩，我們看到當前台灣的兒童詩人作品，包括林武憲、蓉子、楊喚諸人所寫童詩，也都宿含了天地人神四要素，甚至凡是國小、國中課本裡頭的童詩，也都如此。因為當前世界，童詩在各國各民族各地區都非常普遍。因此，你不能說，當前的科技世界裡完全不存在著海德格所謂的「詩意」，其實仍然存在。

　　這麼說，應該把童詩當成海德格所謂「詩意」作品的原型

來看，換句話說，兒童世界，「詩意」永遠與我們同在，有待長大成人後，將這種「詩意」擴大表現成一種大自然的詩來看待。

因此，海德格所謂的「詩意」以及「詩意」的價值，就是李秀兒童詩的「詩意」以及「詩意」的價值。

然而，李秀的28首童詩，有一、兩首並不是寫這種「詩意」的。例外的一、兩首裡，她寫這種詩意的棲居喪失。也就是說，詩人也看到兒童喪失詩意棲居的可能性。此時，這個兒童，目睹環境的殘酷面，它會從詩意的棲居中忽然墜落下來，成為焦慮、不安、恐懼的孩子，一如被趕離伊甸園的亞當夏娃，它立即陷身於災難的世界之中。比如看到父母可能離婚的這件悲慘事件，它受到極大困擾。這時它想到死亡，想到用死亡來逃避一切。它開始體會焦慮、死亡，此時的兒童就喪失「詩意的棲居」「真理」「一」「澄明之境」而墜落到早期海德格所說的必有一死的存在困境中了。可見詩人心目中兒童，不是單純只會置身於「一」世界中的生靈，它偶而也會墜落。假如要分析這一、兩首詩，就要花掉更多文字，因此，不想再分析，只將當中一首詩原文陳列於下，當成本文的結束：

冤家

阿母若拭目屎若講
若無為著囝伊袂留伫厝
阿爸氣噗噗大聲喝起來
若無後生伊早就離開矣

每擺怹若為著代誌相冤家
就操來操去講攏是為著我
我變成怹負擔的糞埽物
我定定想欲按怎辦較好

阿爸參阿母閣冤家起來矣
我足想欲藏起來抑是死去
予怹著急四界攏揣無我
我就毋免煩惱怹欲離婚

※參考書目：
馬丁‧海德格著，孫周興譯：《林中路》（台北，時報文化
出版，1994）
滕守堯著：《海德格》（台北，生智文化，1998）

台文戰線 文學翻譯叢書01

台英雙語童詩集
A Collection of Children's Poems
In Taiwanese and English

一欉小花蕊
A Little Flower

作　　者：李秀 Louise Lee Hsiu
出　版　者：台文戰線雜誌社
地　　址：高雄市鼓山區銘傳路60號
電　　話：0933-636555・0933-636678
　　　　　e-mail:leehsiu@hotmail.com
郵政劃撥：41077199　戶名：李秀
封面繪圖：凃妙沂
封底繪圖：李秀
內頁插畫：蔡八千
英文校對：Barbara Ladouceur
美編印刷：*Anita* 設計印刷工作室
出版日期：2011年2月初版一刷
定　　價：NT $200（in Taiwan）
　　　　　CAD $12（in Canada）
　　　　　US $12（in USA）
國際書碼：ISBN 978-986-85352-3-7

＊購20本以上5折優待，10本以上75折優待。

國家圖書館出版品預行編目資料

一蕊小花蕊嘴：臺英雙語童詩集／李秀作.
--初版.--高雄市：臺文戰線雜誌，2011.02
104面；17X23公分.--(臺文戰線文學翻譯
叢書；1)中英對照
ISBN　978-986-85352-3-7(平裝)

863.59　　　　　　　　　　99026678